the world's longest licorice rope

matt myers

RANDOM HOUSE STUDIO

NEW YORK

Ben found a nickel on the sidewalk.

His dad said he could earn twenty nickels an hour
raking leaves, so Ben got two more nickels from that.

He traded a carved stick
for three more nickels.

The sofa gave him another nickel.

And the neighbor paid him seven nickels to paint his fence!

Now Ben had a bagful of nickels.

He took them to the neighborhood treat fair,
but there were so many goodies, he wasn't sure what to get.

Until he saw a sign for the
world's longest licorice rope.
And it only cost one nickel!

world's longest
licorice rope
one nickel

"Just how long is it?" Ben asked.

"How long is the world?"
a girl said.

Ben didn't know.
But he was hungry enough to find out.
He chewed until he came to a river.

Fortunately, a girl was renting boats.

Ben got stuck in the snow.

A girl was selling snowshoes for one nickel.
Each.

Later, Ben noticed a lion staring at him in an impolite way.

Luckily, a girl was renting . . . carrot suits?

"Lions are carnivorous," she said.
"They would never eat a vegetable.
 Or licorice."

"I hope this works," Ben said in his best carrot accent.

Eventually, Ben bumped into a pyramid.
It looked steep, but at least no one was asking for nickels.

Ben kept chewing until he got to the edge of a cliff.

"I'm tired," Ben said.

"I'm Jimmy."

"I have the world's longest licorice rope," Ben said.

"No, *I* have the world's longest licorice rope," said Jimmy.

"Hey! Did you sell us the same licorice rope?"

"We both paid you for it?"

"Correct. See how much you have in common?
Now, for just one nickel each,
you can be friends!"

"Pay?"

"To be friends?"

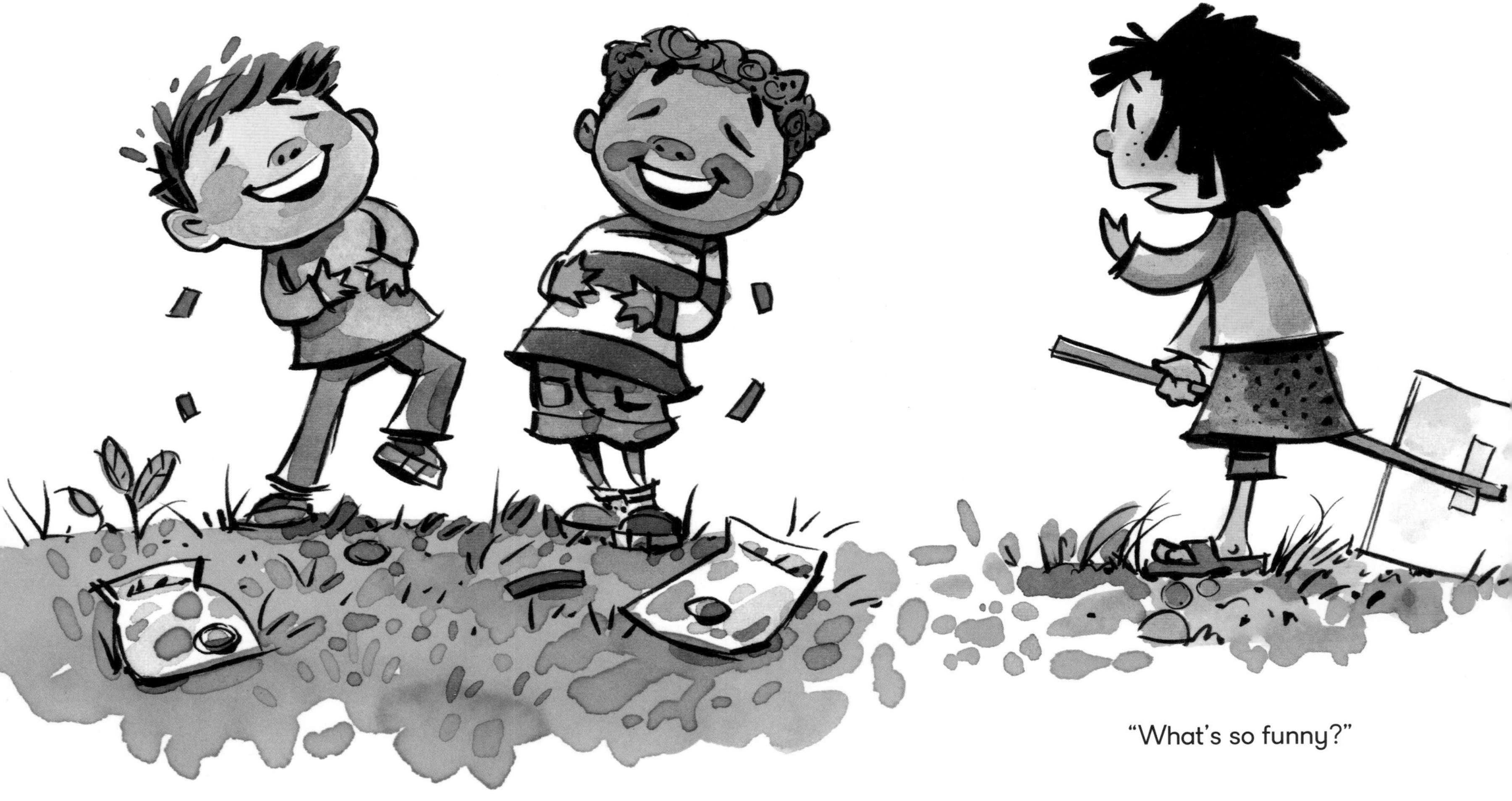

"What's so funny?"

"Friends are free!"

For all the children who follow their curiosity

All rights reserved. Published in the United States by Random House Studio,
an imprint of Random House Children's Books, a division of Penguin Random House LLC,
New York.

Random House Studio with colophon is a trademark of Penguin Random House LLC.

Visit us on the Web! rhcbooks.com

Educators and librarians, for a variety of teaching tools, visit us at RHTeachersLibrarians.com

Library of Congress Cataloging-in-Publication Data is available upon request.
ISBN 978-0-593-18001-3 (trade) — ISBN 978-0-593-18002-0 (lib. bdg.) —
ISBN 978-0-593-18003-7 (ebook)

The artist used watercolor dyes and ink to create the illustrations for this book.
The text of this book is set in 12-point Granary.
Interior design by Nicole Gastonguay

MANUFACTURED IN CHINA

10 9 8 7 6 5 4 3 2 1

First Edition